KANGA RAID

CHRIS GLATTE

KANGA RAID

Severn River Publishing
www.SevernRiverBooks.com

ISBN: 978-1-64875-270-4 (Paperback)

ALSO BY CHRIS GLATTE

Tark's Ticks Series

Tark's Ticks

Valor's Ghost

Gauntlet

Valor Bound

Dark Valley

War Point

A Time to Serve Series

A Time to Serve

The Gathering Storm

The Scars of Battle

164th Regiment Series

The Long Patrol

Bloody Bougainville

Bleeding the Sun

Operation Cakewalk (Novella)

Standalone Novel

Across the Channel

To find out more about Chris Glatte and his books, visit

severnriverbooks.com/authors/chris-glatte

1

WARM WELCOME

Lieutenant Willoth stood on the deck of the SS *Taroona* and caught his first glimpse of his destination—Port Moresby on the west coast of Papua New Guinea. He thought they'd never arrive. The over one thousand kilometer trip from Townsville, Queensland, took longer than normal. The convoy zigzagged its way across the Coral Sea to throw off the genuine threat posed by Japanese submarines.

The commander of the 2/5th Independent Company, Major Murdock, kept the men's minds off the threat with daily vigorous training. The men grumbled, but Lt. Willoth, commanding Third Section of Third Platoon, happily complied. He'd worked too hard at the Australian Army Special Warfare School in Wilson's Point, Victoria, to simply relax and lose his edge. Especially now that they were finally getting into the war.

Port Moresby shimmered in the morning light. The color of the water changed from deep blue to light green and aqua. The water sparkled in the April sunshine.

They disembarked soon after docking. The men marched in single file along the docks. Willoth watched them proudly.

The arduous six-week commando course they'd all gone through pitted them against harsh natural conditions and a cruel, unforgiving training cadre. The shared experience bonded them all, despite their differing ranks.

He heard a siren blaring from somewhere inland and stopped, searching for the source. The men kept marching. A regular Australian Imperial Force trooper, or AIF, yelled at them, "Air raid! Get to cover!"

For a moment, Willoth didn't know what to do. His mind didn't want to process the information. He'd only just arrived. He yelled, "Get off the docks and find cover."

The men broke ranks and hustled along the pier. The AIF trooper pointed. "Over there. Head to the bunker."

Willoth stopped beside the trooper and waved his men forward. "Come on, lads. Move it." He followed his section toward a large sandbagged structure. Men wearing various combinations of uniforms converged at the doorways and squeezed inside. Willoth was reminded of ants streaming back to their mounds during a sudden rainstorm.

He followed the last man of his section inside. Lieutenant Blakely's men from Second Section came next. Willoth barked orders, "Move to the back and find seats where you can." He pushed himself against the wall to allow more men to stream past.

Lieutenant Blakely ducked his six-foot-five body into the enclosure. He addressed his friend and fellow section leader. "Wouldn't you know it, we finally get out of the hold of that rust bucket and we have to squeeze in somewhere worse."

Willoth slapped his back. "Not to worry, if we're lucky we'll get Jap bombs soon."

Blakely leaned close. "I didn't see any planes, did you?"

Willoth shook his head. "Might be a false alarm."

A nearby dock worker dressed in shabby clothes that

looked more oil than fabric said, "Japs bomb us nearly every day. It's not a false alarm."

Blakely scowled and nodded. "They ever hit anything?"

The dock worker shrugged. "Sometimes. Especially when they see a fat target like that troop transport sitting on the docks."

Willoth chimed in, his voice laced with worry. "That's our boat. We haven't even offloaded it yet."

Blakely added, "Wouldn't that beat all? Lose our supplies before we can step off."

The air in the enclosed space became stiflingly unpleasant. A buzzing noise outside made the dock worker point to the ceiling. "Hear that?" Willoth strained and heard what sounded like many airplane engines overhead. The dock worker scoffed, "Not a false alarm."

Anti-aircraft batteries opened fire. The tremendous noise made him think there must be hundreds of them. The whistling of bombs falling from on high cut through the 40mm Bofors fire and made them all cringe and duck lower.

Thumping explosions shook the ground. Dust and dirt descended from the ceiling and choked them. The explosions rocked the shelter, and Willoth imagined the bombs must be dropping right on top of them. For his men to die before they'd even fired a shot in anger didn't seem fair. The bombs kept shaking the ground. He thought it would never end.

Finally, the explosions tapered and stopped. The anti-aircraft fire also stopped, and the silence hung heavily in the dust-filled air. Men coughed and hacked. The dock worker took off his hat and slapped it against his leg. "That wasn't bad. Short one. We weren't their target." He stood and moved to the heavy canvas door flap. He pushed it open and peered outside, then back into the shelter. "Careful, sometimes Zeros follow the bombers with strafing runs." The din of the air-raid siren continued. The dock worker left, leaving the flap swaying in his wake.

Willoth exchanged a glance with Blakely. Blakely shrugged. "Don't wanna stay in here any longer than we have to."

Willoth nodded his agreement. "Me either." He raised his voice and announced, "All right, let's get out of here. Watch for enemy Zeros, though."

Lt. Blakely had his pistol out as he pushed through the flap, and his men followed. Willoth waited for his men, then led them outside. Smoke and dust wafted through the air and cut the sun's rays considerably.

Willoth searched for the bomb damage and saw that the dock worker's assessment was accurate. The docks were untouched. Smoke rose from the west, near the airstrip. He saw planes darting through the smoke and for a moment thought they were Zeros. Upon closer inspection, he realized they were Australian P-40 Kittyhawks. He wondered if they'd tried to intercept the bombers or simply vacated the airfield to avoid being destroyed on the ground.

He stuffed his pistol back into the holster and snapped it shut. The men searched the skies nervously. Willoth saw more men emerging from various shelters, but none of them were part of his company and few were soldiers. He strode to Lt. Blakely's side. "Siren's still wailing. Maybe we should go back inside."

Blakely shook his head. "I don't think—"

He was interrupted by the sudden appearance of four Kittyhawks flying low and fast overhead. The engines roared, and all four pulled up in steep climbs at the same moment. The power and grace brought a smile to Willoth's face. He watched them climb away and turn back the way they'd come. He wondered what they were up to.

Private Stoneman, a rifleman in Willoth's section, pointed and shouted, "Zeros!" He pulled his Lee-Enfield off his shoulder and chambered a round.

Anti-aircraft fire erupted again, but this time the smaller, close-in weapons. A trooper manning a heavy .50-caliber machine gun in a heavily sandbagged gun pit opened fire behind him. The .50 wasn't standard, and he briefly wondered if it was an American crew. Willoth ducked and peered behind him, seeing large tracer rounds chasing four streaking Zeros. The tracers fell well behind the enemy planes.

Some men in the company had seen combat in Africa fighting the Germans. None of them, however, had seen an enemy Japanese. The four Zeros flew only a couple hundred feet off the ground, and Willoth couldn't stop staring. They looked almost majestic.

He'd overheard pilots talking about the vaunted Zero. They considered it a nearly unstoppable fighter when flown by a skilled pilot. The planes could out-climb and out-turn anything the Allies had. The only advantage the heavier Kitty-hawks had was their ability to dive away and to take damage and keep flying. The four low-flying Kittyhawks would have their hands full if the Zeros went after them.

The Zeros opened fire, and the sound reminded Willoth of a buzzsaw. The ground a hundred yards away erupted with massive geysers of black dirt. Bright tracer rounds struck, sparked, and zinged back into the sky. A parked truck erupted in flames as the tightly packed barrels of fuel in the back exploded. A black pall of smoke and fire lifted into the sky.

Willoth ducked back into the trench leading to the shelter but didn't go back inside. He couldn't tear himself away from watching the destruction. One of Blakely's soldiers extended the bipod of his Bren gun and took aim, but the Zeros arced up and extended out of range before he could fire. The Zeros left a path of carnage and destruction in their wakes. They disappeared around the backside of a nearby hill. The anti-aircraft fire dropped off at the same time.

Willoth wondered if the Zeros would tangle with the Kitty-hawks. He supposed the Australian pilots had taken themselves out of harm's way and would fight when they had the advantage. The engine noises faded until they were only a memory. The two sections of troopers looked over the burning destruction. The flames from the truck reached fifty feet and showed no signs of diminishing.

Finally, the wailing air-raid siren stopped, and men emerged from bunkers and shelters. They shook themselves and peered warily skyward, like mice searching for circling hawks.

Captain Wilkes, Third Platoon's leader, emerged and smacked his hat against his leg. He noticed Willoth and Blakely's men with their weapons out and ready. He stomped toward them, and Willoth, Blakely, and the enlisted men snapped to attention. Wilkes straightened his arms and fumed, "Why were you out of cover? Are you trying to get your men killed?"

Willoth stared straight ahead and blurted, "No excuse, sir."

Wilkes's jaw rippled, and he pushed his powerful chest into Lt. Blakely. Blakely towered over him but was no less intimidated. He finally shouted, "No excuse, sir."

Wilkes stepped away and pressed his fists into his hips and gave his section leaders a once-over. "The siren's there for a reason. You don't leave cover until it stops. Understood?"

They answered in unison, "Yes, sir."

After the air raid, Port Moresby returned to business as usual. Smoke still curled up from the destroyed fuel truck, but the fire had been extinguished. Willoth and Blakely got their men back on track offloading and storing their equipment from the transport. The heat and humidity made the work miserable, but they pushed on and soon had everything offloaded and stowed. The hard work gave them all an appetite, and they moved to the mess hall, hoping to fill the void.

Willoth left the men in the capable hands of Staff Sergeant Umberson. He led them to a large nearby mess hall. Willoth entered an adjacent building along with other hungry officers. On his way there, he marveled at how many different uniforms he encountered. US infantrymen, US Army Air Corps, both navies as well as merchant marines, AIF soldiers, and pilots wandered the streets. He could feel the tension in the air, as though everyone expected a Japanese invasion force to show up any second.

Despite having gone through six weeks of commando training, Willoth and the rest of the company assumed they'd be used to help garrison Port Moresby and defend it from the expected push by the Japanese. He doubted they'd get to put any of their unusual talents, besides maybe sharpshooting, to the test.

The smell wafting from the mess hall curbed their appetites substantially. Willoth couldn't decide which was worse, the cabbage or the Bully Beef. Combining the two made the most sense, but no one left feeling satiated.

They retired to their barracks, a long wooden structure that had seen better days, and Willoth and Blakely compared notes on the day's events.

"Any casualties?" asked Willoth.

Blakely shook his head. "An AIF bloke said no one was hurt. I guess no one was in the truck that blew sky high."

Willoth nodded. "It's still burning, or at least smoking. No one seems too worried about it."

"Happens every day. Sometimes twice a day. Japs come all the way from Rabaul."

Willoth whistled, recalling a map he'd pored over daily for weeks, memorizing Papua New Guinea and its surroundings. "That's a long flight."

"That's why we got an early warning. They fly over a lot of observers. I hear the coast watchers are worth their weight in gold around here."

"Probably a good idea to know where the bomb shelters are."

Blakely nodded. "Already got the routes memorized. Haven't heard about any night raids, but you never know."

"Think the Japs'll invade? I mean Port Moresby?"

Blakely finished folding his last tee shirt and placed it neatly into his footlocker. He let the lid shut with a loud bang, making a few officers glare. "Port Moresby's the key to New Guinea. If the Japs get the port and the airfields, the next stop's bloody Australia. Yeah, I think they'll make a go at it. What d'you think?"

"Suppose so." Willoth shrugged. "Glad to be doing our bit. You know—for King and country and all that."

Blakely agreed. "Makes more sense to be here fighting the Nips than in bloody Africa fighting the Krauts."

"Sure be nice to use the skills we picked up in Victoria." He paused. "But I don't see that happening repelling a Jap landing force."

Blakely said, "You never know. Maybe they'll put us to work with the demos somehow."

"More likely sniping work."

"They'll put us wherever we're needed. Maybe we'll clean the dishes." Willoth gave him a pained look. Blakely explained, "Truth is, the brass doesn't know what to do with blokes like us. We're not exactly infantry. We don't fit into a nice round hole, and I think they'd rather we did. We'll probably get rolled into another company or kept in reserve. In other words, we're experimental, and it's anyone's guess what happens next..."

2

MISSION ORDER

April gave way to May, and the threat from the Japanese became more than just a threat. Port Moresby buzzed with activity. Hasty fortifications went up along the likely Japanese amphibious landing points. From sunrise to sundown, 2/5th Independent Company worked alongside various other troopers, filling and stacking sandbags.

A feeling of dread hung over the town like a black pall. The air raids continued nearly every day, keeping them on edge and sometimes destroying work they'd spent all day on in an instant of violence and flame. Some men died, others maimed forever.

Rumors of an approaching Japanese landing force constantly circulated. Finally, on May 4th, the rumors weren't just rumors anymore. The alert status elevated to high. Nimble fighters rose from the airfield to rendezvous with B-17s taking off from airfields in Australia. They returned with stories of heavy naval engagements just over the horizon.

For a few days, the air raids on Port Moresby ceased. At night, they could see distant flashes, as though they were watching mysterious sheet lightning. During the day, they saw innocuous-looking plumes of distant smoke. Port Moresby remained tense and vigilant. The inexorable, undefeated Japanese juggernaut had them in their sights.

The dark mood lifted a few days later when the news came that the Allies had turned the Japanese force back. At first, no one believed it, or they thought it was propaganda or wishful thinking. Perhaps the Japanese started the rumor to trick the defenders into dropping their guard. But soon the eyewitness accounts from shot-up bomber crews forced to use Port Moresby for an emergency airfield couldn't be denied. They'd seen burning carriers and ships from both sides, but they'd also seen the Japanese leaving the area. By mid-May, no one clung to the idea of a Japanese amphibious landing of Port Moresby.

Willoth and the other soldiers of the 2/5th Independent Company had settled into their new environs. The food was terrible; they lost weight, and some needed to be hospitalized for malaria and other tropical diseases. Willoth and the other untested officers grumbled that they'd never get a chance to see combat.

A nervous corporal stuck his head into the officers' quarters and saluted. Lieutenant Wilson, a burly soldier nearly as wide as he was tall, barked, "What is it, Corporal? Out with it."

The corporal stammered, "Yes, sir. Captain Wilkes wants all officers in his hut at 1400 hours."

Wilson squinted and growled, "What's it all about?"

The corporal gulped and shook his head. "I—I don't know, sir," he stammered.

Wilson nodded and shooed him away as though brushing off a fly, then turned to the others. "Maybe we're finally getting a mission."

The officers of the 2/5th Independent Company sat inside the swelteringly hot Quonset hut, awaiting Major Murdock. The open side windows and overhead fans barely moved the stifling air. Lieutenant Willoth drained the lukewarm water in his canteen. He hoped the major would get there soon, or he'd need to step outside for a refill.

Lieutenant Colonel Fleay entered, followed by the major. Willoth and the other officers bolted to their feet as though electrocuted. Colonel Fleay held out his hands. "At ease, men. As you were."

The officers sat on their rickety chairs as an aide unveiled a large map pinned onto a corkboard. The map showed Papua New Guinea with Port Moresby front and center. A general murmur arose from the ranks. Maps, particularly detailed maps like the one before them, were rare. New Guinea's wilds, although populated with natives, hadn't been mapped extensively by Western powers. It posed a major problem when trying to plan operations.

Fleay's high, angular cheekbones and deep-set brown eyes grinned at the assembled men. "Don't get too excited. The map's still not what it should be. But for our purposes, it'll have to do." There were a few chuckles near the front. He picked up a pointer stick and smacked an area near the northeastern coast. "Lae," he moved the pointer south, "and Salamaua are occupied by the Nips. The New Guinea Volunteer Rifles, or NGVRs, were pushed out when the enemy arrived. But they maintain stations in the village of Wau," he smacked a spot inland from Salamaua, "Mubo, and Bulol. They watch the Japs at Lae and Salamaua and report their activities to us regularly." He looked the men over, then continued. "They've been asking for reinforcements so they can attack. They're confident that hit-and-run tactics would impede the Japs' progress building airstrips." He readjusted his pointer on

Wau. "Wau has an airfield. It's rough, but C-47s can get in and out. It's how we've kept the NGVRs supplied all this time. It's a relatively short flight, but weather often shuts it down. Now that we've stopped the Nips in the Coral Sea, MacArthur and Blameley think Lae and Salamaua are going to become important jump-off points. They want us to take them back." He paused as the men looked at one another and murmured among themselves. Fleay held up his hands for quiet. "I know, I know. We're just a company." He lifted his chin. "We'll be their eyes on the ground. We'll find attack lanes, vulnerabilities, and whatnot, so by the time we fly in a larger force, they'll be able to get in and attack quickly.

"The Yanks will help with the airlift into Wau. From what I hear, it's a bit hairy. We fly through a gap in the Owen Stanleys, then a bit of an up-and-down to the airfield. You've got two days to gather gear and supplies. We leave on the twenty-fourth if the weather holds." He shifted the pointer stick behind his back and looked over the sea of perspiring faces. "Major Murdock will fill you in on the specifics." He stepped away from the table, and the men got to their feet. Fleay added, "One more thing. Command is calling us the Kanga Force." He smiled, and his caterpillar mustache twitched on his upper lip. "I rather like it. Has a nice ring to it."

Lieutenant Willoth held on tight to the metal bench sticking from the side of the C-47's skin. His section of twelve men were crammed in side by side with Lt. Blakely's section. Blakely sat directly across from him but kept his eyes shut tight. Willoth tried that but immediately felt queasy as the plane buffeted through the erratic, violent turbulence.

He chanced a peek out the small, dirty window and saw

dense fog. The plane dropped like a stone, and his seat belt strap cut into his hips and thighs painfully as his body tried to hit the ceiling. The plane jolted hard, as though hitting something solid, then rose suddenly, pushing him into the seat. It felt like the wings would snap off. He glimpsed heavy jungle through the small window. It looked much closer than he thought it should.

He leaned forward and saw both pilots gripping the yokes and controls. He could see beyond them through the cockpit windscreen. It didn't help. It looked like they were headed straight for the jungle. The plane steadied, and he continued watching. They weaved through a gap not much wider than the wingspan.

The plane had no supplemental oxygen, and some of the surrounding peaks reached as high as thirteen thousand feet. They flew through a well-travelled gap in the mountains that kept them below seven thousand feet.

He forced himself back into his seat. He stared straight ahead. Blakely still had his damned eyes shut and actually looked like he might be asleep. Willoth shook his head, sure his friend's antics were for show. He couldn't wait to smack him when they landed.

Suddenly the pilots' excited chatter cut through the droning dual engines. So far, they hadn't spoken much, which Willoth preferred. He leaned forward and saw them gesturing and pointing upward. Next thing he knew, the plane dove and turned hard left. The engines screamed, and he could feel the plane picking up speed. Blakely's eyes snapped open, and he looked as scared as Willoth felt.

The plane snapped the other direction and tilted toward ninety degrees. Willoth hung from his single strap, staring down at Blakely, as though he were hanging from the ceiling. Despite the violent maneuvering, no one shouted or called out in fear. They were too busy hanging on. Finally, they straightened out and flew level. The engines changed back to a more normal pitch. When Willoth caught his breath and knew he wouldn't throw up, he leaned forward and yelled toward the cockpit, "What the bloody hell happened, mate?"

The copilot leaned away from his controls, lifted one side of his headphones, and asked, "What?"

"What the bloody hell was that all about?"

The American copilot grinned. "Sorry. A flight of Zeros flew over us. Had to dive into a canyon to avoid them seeing us." Willoth felt the blood leave his face, and he felt nauseous. The copilot gave him a thumbs-up and grinned. "They didn't see us. Smooth sailing from here on out."

Willoth leaned back and shut his eyes. He murmured to himself, "Bloody Yanks."

Fifteen minutes later, the engine pitch changed again and he felt the plane slow noticeably. He peeked out the window and saw a few structures through the wafting mists. To the south, there was a short dirt strip of land. It looked like a farmer's plowed field, but the pathetically hanging windsock at the edge told him it was their destination. It looked impossibly short and narrow.

He leaned forward and saw the pilots adjusting themselves in their seats, as though getting ready for a difficult maneuver. Bloody hell, he thought. He waved to get Blakely's attention and pointed out the window. He yelled over the engine's roar, "Coming into Wau." He pointed at the pilots. "Yanks weren't as nervous about the bloody Zeros as they are about landing."

Blakely shook his head and glanced at the other commandos. Most gripped their seats or had death grips on their seat belts. "We'll be all right."

The plane turned sharply, dropped fast, then leveled

and seemed to skate sideways. Willoth couldn't keep himself from leaning forward. He saw the approaching airfield and thought he might be hallucinating. It looked as though they were pointed straight into the ground, but his body told him they were flat and level. At the last possible instant, the nose lifted drastically and he felt the front wheels bounce onto the dirt. The engines roared, and the tail wheel touched down. It felt as though they were climbing a steep hill.

They bounced along for a few hundred yards before the pilots whipped the plane around with a sudden burst of brakes, engine, and rudder. Willoth thought perhaps they'd hit something, but when they'd stopped turning, the copilot leaned over and yelled, "Everybody out! Now!"

The roar of the engines diminished but didn't stop. Blakely, nearest the door, unbuckled his waist strap and opened the door with a flourish of sound and wind. Daylight streamed in as though a dam had broken, and Willoth got his first smell of Wau. It wasn't unpleasant—like recently tilled earth.

He struggled to unfasten his seat belt. Blakely was already out, and his section of troopers followed. Willoth's troopers unstrapped their packs and gear and passed everything forward. Willoth slung his rifle over one shoulder and his pack over the other and shambled off the plane.

Once they'd emptied the plane, the copilot opened his side window and yelled, "That everything?"

Willoth nodded and returned the thumbs-up sign. The pilot gave a cursory salute and a sideways grin. The engines roared, the brakes released, and the plane shot down the steeply sloped airstrip. It arced gracefully into the morning sky and was soon out of sight. As they cleared the area, another C-47 emerged and lined up on the airstrip.

They watched the successful uphill landing. Willoth shook his head. "I'll be happy if I never have to do that again...ever."

Lieutenant Blakely slapped his shoulder. "Hell, that was nothing. My dad flew a little single engine in the bush. This here's like an international airport, far as I'm concerned."

"That why you were pretending to sleep?"

He guffawed. "Pretending? Nah, airplane engines put me to sleep. My mum says Dad used to take me up when I was fussy as a baby. Worked every time."

Willoth wasn't convinced. "You're full of shit, mate. I saw your face when we evaded those Zeros."

Blakely balked, "I thought you were going to puke on me. Now that"—he scowled—"I can't stomach."

They moved away from the edge of the airfield and entered the tiny town of Wau. There were shacks here and there, and a few dirt tracks crisscrossed the area. The locals' black skin shimmered in the morning heat. They greeted the newcomers with smiles and waves. A short white man stepped forward. He was dressed in civilian clothes, but the Lee-Enfield rifle slung over his shoulder and the patch on his breast told them he was with the NGVR.

"Hallo," he called. "Welcome to Wau." He spread his arms expansively. "I'm sure you'll find your stay with us as pleasant as eating shit spread on toast."

Willoth and Blakely exchanged surprised looks and approached him. "Pardon me?" Willoth said.

The volunteer braced but didn't salute. Upon first inspection, Willoth thought he was a young man, but there was something about his eyes and the deep crow's feet that aged him. Willoth asked, "What's that about shit on toast?"

The volunteer grinned. "You've gotta have a bloody sense of humor out here, mate. I'm Erwin Plansky." The second plane roared off the runway, clearing the way for another C-47 just turning onto short final. "You picked a good day. Fog's been thick the last few days."

Willoth nodded. "We'll get the entire company in by the looks of it. Our flight had to dodge a few Zeros on the way in." The revelation didn't faze Plansky at all.

Blakely indicated the surrounding hills. "We need to worry about snipers?"

Plansky shook his head. "Japs can't make a move into our valley without us knowing 'bout it. Suppose one or two could sneak through, but that hasn't happened yet. I'll wager you're as safe here as you were in Port Moresby."

Willoth nodded and relaxed his stance a little. "The brass will be here soon. Can you show us where to put our kit?"

The sound of an automobile grinding from first to second gear made them turn. A beat-up pickup truck bounced and weaved along the main dirt track.

Plansky smiled. "Here comes old Grimerson now."

Willoth noticed a gray-haired man leaning over the steering wheel. "That the truck's name or the driver?"

Plansky replied, "The driver. Truck's name is Roo. But it's lost most of its bounce." He laughed. "Can't say the same for Captain Grimerson, though. He's been here longer than any of us. He helped build this town, and he's still as spry as any one of us younger sods."

The truck pulled up beside them and stopped with grinding brakes. Captain Grimerson of the NGVR pushed his shoulder into the door, and it squeaked as it opened, as though in pain. Grimerson pushed the emergency brake, and it ratcheted into place. Before stepping from the cab, he hesitated, making sure the old truck wouldn't roll.

Finally, he stepped out and smiled at the two officers. Willoth and Blakely braced, and Captain Grimerson looked them up and down, then said, "Hello and welcome to the

Bulol Valley." Willoth and Blakely both thanked him, and Grimerson continued. "Not sure what you blokes did to deserve this assignment, but we're glad to have you."

Willoth immediately liked Grimerson and smiled back. "We're happy to be here, sir. We can finally put our training to use."

Grimerson nodded and stroked his cleft chin sagely. "Yes, commandos, no less." He punched Plansky's arm. "Told you they didn't forget about us. We're moving up in the world. It'll be nice to see some fresh faces—and supplies." Willoth noticed Plansky's smile fade and his eyes darken. Grimerson ordered, "Take old Roo to the airfield. I'll show them to their quarters."

Plansky nodded. "Yes, sir." He hopped into the truck, and the door complained noisily as he pulled it shut.

Grimerson held out his arm. "It's this way. Don't get too comfortable though, I expect we'll be sending you out to meet the Nips soon enough."

3

TRAP

The string of C-47s continued uninterrupted until the entire company arrived safely on the ground. Lieutenant Colonel Fleay came in on the last plane. Major Murdock had landed in the middle of the pack and quickly sorted out where the company would set up shop.

When Colonel Fleay strolled off the plane along with the last section of 2/5th Independent Company, he quickly asserted control. He approached Captain Grimerson of the NGVRs, and they exchanged salutes. Fleay gave him the once-over, clearly unimpressed, then offered a tight grin. "I'm Colonel Fleay. I'll be taking over command here, and that includes the NGVR cadre."

Grimerson nodded. "Yes, sir. I got the word. We're now named Kanga Force, and we're under your command."

"Quite right. How many of your men left today?"

Grimerson lifted his chin. "Two wounded men went out. None of the others wanted to leave. I have forty-one Volunteer Rifles left, sir."

Fleay looked surprised. "Your men know they can leave?"

Grimerson answered, "Yes, sir. Of course. But this area is

their home. We've been here since the start. No reason to leave now. I had to order the two wounded men onto the plane with the promise they could return when their wounds healed."

"Miners?" Fleay asked.

Grimerson pursed his lips, then responded, "Before the Nips arrived, yes, sir. We haven't had much time for mining ever since, but as soon as we kick Tojo out, we'll get back to it. This land is full of gold." He took in a deep breath through his nose and let it out with a flourish. "You can almost smell it."

The edges of Fleay's mouth turned down. "All I smell is rot. I'll need to set up a command post." He looked at the ramshackle buildings with obvious disgust.

Grimerson pointed toward the center of town. "Your Major Kneer has already seen to that, sir." He extended his arm. "I can lead you there and fill you in on what we're facing."

Fleay shook his head. "I'd like to get set up first. Come to the CP in two hours."

"Yes, sir."

Fleay followed Grimerson, and when he'd shown him the building, Fleay said, "Get cleaned up before you arrive, Captain. Dismissed."

Grimerson's grin hid his seething anger. Sergeant Plansky stepped forward and spit into the mud. "He's quite the lovely man, isn't he?"

"Thought these commando types weren't quite so stiff, but I was obviously mistaken."

"Kanga Force, sir?"

Grimerson smiled. "Kanga Force. Right. Management loves their pet names." He dusted off his tunic. "This *is* my best uniform top, and I shaved a few hours ago."

Plansky shook his head. "Guess they'll have to learn the hard way."

Grimerson shrugged. "It's a steep learning curve out here.

They'll adapt." He grinned. "They'll have to. At least now our pleas for supplies won't go unanswered. Doubt Colonel Fleay will put up with being ignored."

Plansky nodded. "That'll be a welcome change. The men are already enjoying the food and ogling all the ammunition and new toys. The commandos don't travel light. They even brought mortars and plenty of ammo for 'em, too."

Grimerson brushed the hair from his eyes. "Maybe we'll finally be able to do more than just watch the little buggers."

A week after flying into Wau airfield, Lieutenant Willoth found himself perched on a wooden platform suspended in a large tree overlooking the Japanese-occupied town of Salamaua. Despite his training, weaving through the deep valleys and up the steep mountains on tracks no wider than a footprint in spots made for a harrowing experience. The NGVR men leading them barely broke a sweat.

Mist clung to the ground, but through the high-powered binoculars, he saw enemy soldiers milling about. Natives mixed with them, some working on Japanese projects, others tending crops and fields. The majority worked on the dirt airfield at the edge of town. The work looked backbreaking. Everything had to be done by hand. The natives cut and hacked trees using saws, axes, and machetes. Animals pulled various equipment over and through the dirt, smoothing, leveling, and extending the edges.

Willoth handed the binoculars off to Captain Wilkes. "Looks like they're extending it."

Wilkes took another look and nodded. "Probably want to use it for bombers. It's a short flight to Port Moresby from there. Not to mention Wau and Bulol."

Willoth pointed and stated excitedly, "Look at that. I didn't see 'em before. Jap Zeros."

Wilkes focused on the spot. Japanese soldiers near the edge of the jungle pulled camouflage netting, exposing two green-painted Zeros. The red meatballs along the fuselage and on each wing were obvious, even without the binoculars. "Well, I'll be damned. First enemy planes I've seen that weren't bombing or strafing us."

Willoth searched the sky. Sunlight shone through here and there, but thick puffy clouds hid most of the sky. "Sure be a good time for a bombing run."

Wilkes nodded and scanned more of the airfield. "Haven't seen our aviators for a few days. Wonder when those two snuck in?"

Corporal Nance, an NGVR soldier, shook his head. "We've had this place under observation for months. Either they came in at night and we missed 'em, or they offloaded 'em and put 'em together here."

He wore a ring of weaved grasses around his head. That, combined with his thick, unwieldy beard, made Willoth think he looked like a crazy man. "Do they do that? Build them here, I mean?"

Nance shrugged. "Haven't actually seen it, but they're sneaky buggers. Wouldn't put anything past them. There've been plenty of small ships in and out of Lae and here. They coulda offloaded them at night and we wouldn't be the wiser."

Captain Wilkes shook his head. "That'd be a lot more trouble than it's worth. Probably flew 'em in from Rabaul. Maybe they're fixing to hit Wau."

They watched as the Japanese pushed both Zeros onto the dirt airstrip. Nance added, "We've seen plenty of float planes land off the beach, but this is the first time I've seen the airstrip being used by fighters. Sometimes they'll bring in one of those small reconnaissance planes, but they can land on a postage stamp."

Wilkes continued scanning the area. He focused and stated, "Looks like the pilots are approaching." He handed the binoculars to Willoth. Nance had his own set. It was an older model, but Nance babied them, keeping the vital piece of equipment in tip-top shape.

Willoth found the two pilots. They exuded confidence even from this distance. "Bloody cocky little shits, aren't they?"

Nance guffawed. "That they are. Before we ran too low on ammunition, we plugged a few of 'em down there."

Willoth pulled the binoculars off his eyes and looked at the scraggly volunteer. "Bet they didn't like that one bit."

Nance smiled, showing off yellowed and chipped teeth. He shook his head. "Like kicking a bloody ant hill. They went berserk. We had to lie low for days while they swept the area." He grinned evilly. "Then we did it again the next week, only this time we put down booby traps." His expression changed. He looked wistfully toward the horizon of the shimmering sea. "Bloody beautiful listening to their screams."

Willoth exchanged a worried glance with Captain Wilkes, who just shook his head and kept watching the pilots. "They don't seem too nervous now," he stated.

Nance looked dejected. "We ran out of munitions. We sustained ourselves with Jap gear for a while, but they stopped venturing from their strongholds, so that dried up too."

Wilkes continued watching the pilots saunter toward their steeds sitting proudly at the far end of the runway. "Command wants us to push on Lae and Salamaua. The fact that the airstrip is operational will make them want to even more. You'll hear Jap screams again soon enough, Corporal."

Nance nodded. "Noticed you brought some goodies to play with."

Wilkes grinned. "That we did. We'll move to the airfield this afternoon and set up a few surprises for 'em. Let them know we haven't forgotten about them. Can your men lead us to likely ambush spots?"

Nance smiled like he'd just been given the keys to every bar in Australia. "Yes, sir. We can definitely do that. They don't venture far anymore, but far enough."

Smoke erupted from both Zeros, and the sound of their engines eventually reached them on the perch. "Too bad we can't drop a few mortar rounds on them right about now," Wilkes lamented. "I wanted to bring a few tubes, but Major Murdock wants to keep 'em close to defend Wau."

Nance's smile didn't waver. "Mortars, ambushes...you blokes are a welcome sight all right. About bloody time we give them a bloody nose."

Corporal Nance briefed Willoth and Wilkes on his plan. The troopers of Third Section listened intently. Willoth felt he could trust the grubby NGVR corporal but wouldn't leave him alone with his sister until he knew more about him. Corporal Nance assured them that the Japanese sent out a daily patrol, usually around 1500 hours. He explained how they alternated between two different routes and today would be the closer eastern route. He drew the approximate position in the dirt, suggesting where to ambush and also where they should set their booby traps.

While Willoth and Third Section gathered weapons and ammo, Nance nearly burst with excitement. He shifted from foot to foot like a child waiting to open presents on Christmas morning.

Before stepping off, Captain Wilkes pulled Willoth aside.

"You're in charge of your section, Lieutenant. Pretend I'm not here." Willoth nodded but thought it unlikely he'd be able to pretend his company commander wasn't there.

Willoth busied himself getting ready. He checked and rechecked his gear and watched Sergeant Umberson, his assistant section leader, check the men over meticulously. Finally, it was time to go.

Willoth stepped away to take a leak. He took a deep breath of warm New Guinea air and blew it out slowly. He glanced up at the sky and shook his head. Over the next few hours he would put his training to the test. Doubts crossed his mind. Could he lead these fine men into battle? Could he pull the trigger and end another man's life? Were these his last few hours on Earth? Would he freeze up and let his men down? That last thought scared him the most. Despite all the tough talk during training, the overarching emotion he felt most was fear of failure.

Finally, it was time to go. His men stood behind the NGVR scouts. Willoth saw the benefit of the thatch-weaved grasses they'd strung around their heads. Despite the goofy overall look, the grass broke up their features nicely. Willoth decided he'd learn to make them—if they survived. He shook the negativity from his head and joined his men. "Lead off, Corporal Nance." Nance's grin beamed ear to ear. He slapped his fellow volunteers' backs, and the three of them led the way.

Willoth waited for a few of his men to amble past before falling into the single file line. Captain Wilkes joined a few men behind him. The NGVRs didn't have their weapons off their shoulders, so none of the troopers did either. The scouts led them as though on a Sunday afternoon stroll through a park back home.

The dirt track narrowed as it dropped into the valley. They

navigated treacherous switchbacks, and Willoth wondered how far he'd roll if he tripped.

When they finally made it to the bottom, Nance and the other two NGVRs took their rifles off their shoulders and crouched. They blended perfectly with their surroundings, and again Willoth admired their use of natural camouflage.

Nance whispered, "We'll move slower from here on out. Ambush spot's less than a mile from here." Willoth nodded and passed the information along. He watched the volunteers move silently through the thin jungle. He took pride in his men's stealthy abilities, but Nance and company worked on a different level altogether. Willoth thought he and his section sounded like elephants in comparison, and more than a few times, the NGVRs glanced back with stern looks.

The 2/5th had been in the Wau area for over a week. Willoth thought he knew the sounds of the jungle, but now he felt as though every little sound was new and terrifying.

Sergeant Umberson touched his arm, and Willoth jolted. Umberson had fought the Krauts in Africa and knew his green section leader struggled with fear and doubt. All the new guys did. He smiled and whispered, "Easy does it, Lieutenant." Willoth gave him a curt nod and focused.

Umberson pointed. "Nance wants us to set up over there on that trail. Says we should set our booby traps to the left. The Japs will come from the right. They'll run into the booby traps later."

Willoth felt annoyed. Had he been daydreaming? He hadn't even seen the two men talking. He moved forward and surveyed the prospective ambush site. His training took over. It was good ground. They'd be able to see the enemy coming from a long way off, and there was a clear and easy extraction route. They'd be able to hit the enemy, and if things didn't go as planned, they could disperse and retreat without having to split their forces.

He checked his wristwatch. It was 1400. "Okay. We've got time to set up the traps and lay the ambush." He pointed. "Take Stoneman, Blanche, and Brewster that way." He held up two fingers. "Two traps. Far enough apart to cause maximum damage."

Sergeant Umberson's jaw rippled. "The men know what to do, sir."

Willoth closed his eyes and nodded. He clapped Umberson's shoulder. "Right, right. I know. Get back here soon as you can."

The troopers spread themselves out along the trail in an off-axis L-shape. The Bren gunner, Private Weathers, formed the hinge point and faced directly up the trail.

A few minutes later, the men setting the demolition traps returned and tucked into the line. Willoth wracked his brain. Had he forgotten anything? He shook his head. He had his rifle ready with an extra magazine nearby, but if everything went well, he wouldn't have to use it.

He glanced behind and saw Captain Wilkes staring back at him. Mostly, Willoth *had* forgotten about him. Wilkes gave him a wry grin, and Willoth took it to mean, *Good job.* He knew his job, but getting recognition never hurt.

He checked his watch: fifteen minutes after the Japanese patrol's suspected departure time. If they were coming, it would be soon. He squinted, trying to see any of the NGVR men. He finally found them, but only because they grinned and waved at him from beneath the bushes. "Crazy old sods, every one of 'em," he murmured to himself.

He heard the enemy before he saw them. Indistinct voices and crunching footfalls turned his sweat to ice. His pulse quickened, and his mouth felt as dry as sawdust. He felt the surrounding men stiffen with anticipation. Muzzles leveled, and men pushed cheeks into stocks and peered over their sights. Weathers with the Bren gun would be the first to fire, unless something untoward occurred.

A Japanese soldier stepped around the corner as though on a stroll. His rifle was off his shoulder, but he held it low. He looked down the long pathway leading straight to them. Willoth thought his eyes bore straight into him, but he knew he may as well be invisible. He forced himself to look away. Instructors told him that staring sometimes could set off an adversary's sixth sense. He didn't know if he believed it or not, but he decided now wasn't the time to test the theory.

Six Japanese soldiers in various states of readiness approached. The Japanese closed the gap quickly, barely looking at their surroundings. Willoth watched them come. If his gaze tipped them off now, they wouldn't escape. He marveled at how small they looked. He knew many Japanese were small in stature, but these men looked smaller than most.

He jumped when the Bren gun opened fire. The soldiers on the trail froze for an instant. Private Weathers adjusted quickly and walked his .303 rounds into the lead man, who writhed and shook as the rounds tore into him. His Type 38 rifle splintered in his hand, and he dropped. The man behind him went down in a flourish of bloody mist and bits of skull. The rest of Third Section opened fire, and within a few short seconds, the only movement on the trail came from spasming death throes. The firing stopped as quickly as it began.

Willoth stared, transfixed for an instant. Sergeant Umberson uttered, "Sir."

Willoth jolted and the trance broke. Smoke wafted onto the trail from multiple hissing barrels. All the targets were down. Willoth got to his knees. "Have the bodies checked for documents. Take their weapons and ammo. We need to be moving in five minutes."

Umberson got to his feet and relayed the orders, singling out four men for the job. "Rest of you cover 'em and gather your shit. Nothing gets left behind for the bloody Nips."

Corporal Nance's flushed face appeared beside Willoth. "The Japs'll send a relief force. We could cut them down the same way."

Willoth scowled. "No. We hit them, and now we fade away. Leave 'em guessing. Get ready to lead us back to the ridge, Corporal."

Nance looked dejected but nodded his understanding. Then he grinned. "Got number thirty-two." He flashed the stock of his Lee-Enfield rifle. It had neat rows in sets of five roman numerals.

Willoth shook his head. "That's government-issued kit, you know."

"They can come get it whenever they want it back. They know where I am."

They left the area minutes later. They heard the distant sound of pursuit, yelling mostly. By the time they got back to the ridge, it was silent.

Willoth asked Nance, "Will they follow our track?"

Nance answered, "I hope so, Lieutenant." He turned serious. "I doubt it. Unless they come in force, they know they'll suffer." He added, "There aren't enough of 'em to come in force."

Captain Wilkes stepped into the conversation. "This sort of action might change that."

Nance nodded. "I say let 'em come." He paused and put his hand to his ear. In the distance, a small rumble rolled up to them. "Ah, yes. I believe one of your dirty tricks got stepped on." He jumped and clicked his heels together. "I do love showing them what for again!"

Captain Wilkes and Lieutenant Willoth watched the other NGVRs join in the dancing. Wilkes leaned toward Willoth's ear. "I think they're all gassed out. Been out here too long, I'd say."

Willoth nodded his agreement. "I'm just glad they're on our side."

The dancing continued and Wilkes muttered under his breath, "We'll see what kind of trouble we stirred up."

4

AMBUSHED

Lieutenant Willoth woke minutes before the sun rose. Three days had passed since his section had successfully ambushed the Japanese. Captain Wilkes left with two NGVRs the morning after the ambush. He'd instructed Willoth to hit the Japanese whenever the opportunity arose but added that he shouldn't take untoward chances.

Willoth rolled off the thin blanket and got to his feet. He stretched his back, getting the blood flowing to his extremities. Sergeant Umberson greeted him with a steaming cup of tea. "Morning, Lieutenant."

Willoth took it gratefully, sipped, and shook his head. "I don't know how you do it, Mick. Do you ever sleep?"

Umberson shrugged. "Course I do. Just an early riser, I guess, and tea makes for a good start to the day."

"That it does." Willoth took another sip. "Our food is bland and possibly dangerous, but the tea's excellent."

"Are your bowels acting up again, sir?"

Willoth rubbed his belly. He'd spent a good deal of time the day before hunched over a log, crapping. "Feels better today. But I'm not keen on eating more Bully Beef, I can tell you."

Umberson grinned. "You can give your portion to Nance. I've never seen a man more excited to eat the nasty stuff. Shovels it in as though it were prime rib."

"Anything happen last night?"

Umberson shook his head. "The outpost was quiet."

Willoth took another sip before setting the tea down carefully. "Let's go have a look." He climbed the old scraggly tree to the observation platform. Sergeant Umberson followed.

Corporal Nance greeted them. "Good morning." He lounged in a gently swaying hammock strung off to the side. Thirty feet separated him from the ground.

Willoth shook his head. "I don't know how you manage to sleep in that thing. Aren't you afraid you'll fall out?"

Nance swung his feet over the side, and the hammock swayed over the abyss. He shrugged and leaned dangerously far over the edge, looking down at the rocks and trees he'd land on if he fell. "Nah. Beats sleeping on the ground with all the creepy crawlies." He swung his legs back and forth, and the hammock swung like a swing set at a park. Willoth knew what came next, and he held his breath. Nance launched himself, did a half turn in the air, and landed lightly on the platform. He stood to his full height and grinned. "We going to kill some Japs today?"

Willoth couldn't help smiling. The man thought of nothing else. The sun blazed over the sea, turning the clouds pink, orange, and red. "Beautiful sunrise." He opened the case containing his binoculars and scanned the river and the airfield beyond. Both still lay in shadow, and smoke from cooking fires rose languidly into the air. The two Zeros had flown off and hadn't returned. The only air activity had been bombers passing high overhead on some unknown errand of destruction.

He scanned slowly, then let the binocs hang from the strap around his neck. "Yes, I think it's time we hit them again." Nance smiled. Willoth spoke before Nance had a chance to. "They send out foragers most days."

Nance's smile faded. "You mean villagers?"

"With an escorting soldier, right?"

Nance nodded.

Willoth continued, "I'm not sure why. It exposes the soldier while he's out there."

Nance shrugged. "They don't trust the villagers to bring back all the roots they harvest. Afraid they'll keep some for themselves."

Willoth cocked his head. "How do you know that?"

Nance looked at him as though he'd lost his mind. "'Cause they told me as much."

Willoth exchanged a glance with Umberson, then turned back to Nance. "You've spoken with them? Recently?"

"Not since the ambush, but last week I had a chat with Peron and Symian. They were on their way to Mubo." He grinned. "I've lived here half my life, you know. You tend to meet people." He continued, "Before the Japs came, we got most of our mining supplies from Salamaua. Boats brought supplies, and we'd pay the villagers to haul 'em over the track to Wau and the Black Cat Mine. Or they'd come into Lae and just bring 'em up the Markham Valley, but it's a longer route, and sometimes the river floods and washes out the road."

"Do you think they'd be willing to draw us a map of the Jap defenses in Salamaua?"

Nance's smile went to a thin line, and he scratched his scruffy beard. "It's a bit complicated. This war doesn't mean much to them." He paused and scrunched his brow, then continued. "You should think of them as businessmen. The gold rush brought in a lot of money quickly. The villagers found out what that could mean to them. They went from simple hunter-gatherers to business sharks in less than a generation."

"So you're saying they're for sale? They'll work for the highest bidder?"

"Exactly. If we pay them, they'll give us whatever you ask for." He raised both arms. "But..."

Umberson finished for him. "But they'll turn on you just as quick if the Nips outbid us."

Nance dropped his hands and nodded.

Willoth ground his teeth. "So we can't trust them."

"Not a whit."

"But they're your friends? Don't they know they're better off with us than the Nips?" Willoth asked.

Nance scowled and shook his head. "So far, they're not. Since this whole thing kicked off, the only business deals they've had have been with the Japs. We ran out of money a long time ago. They won't work with us unless we pay 'em."

"So how d'you know about the Jap sentry?" asked Umberson.

Nance shrugged. "Casual conversation. I just asked about it, and they answered."

"So the Japs make them harvest food for them at gunpoint and they still think they're better off?" asked Umberson.

Nance nodded. "I don't think they like that bit, but they're getting paid to work on the airstrip."

Willoth looked alarmed. "So you told them you were watching them from up here? Told them you saw them being guarded?" He opened his arms. "They know about all this?"

Nance looked from one to the other. "Of course they do. It's in their own backyard."

Willoth stammered, "So—so aren't you worried they'll rat you out?"

Nance itched his beard, and the grating noise suddenly repulsed Willoth. Nance finally answered. "We'd see 'em coming."

"But you said yourself, it's their own backyard. You don't think they'd know how to approach without you seeing them?"

Nance shook his head tightly. "I see where you're coming from, but the villagers would do what the Japs paid them to do. If they said, for instance, 'Take us to the observation point so we can kill those bloody Aussies,' they'd do just that, but they wouldn't necessarily do it stealthily. Now, if they said it another way, 'Take us to the observation point without them seeing us,'" he held up a finger, "then I'd worry. But that won't happen. They don't speak the language, and getting that sort of nuance would be nearly impossible. It's the same reason it hasn't happened yet. The Japs don't know how to ask."

Willoth sat on the edge of the platform and watched the mists rise from the river. Construction on the airfield continued unhindered. He rubbed the back of his neck and his hand came away wet and dirty. "So, if we continue hitting the Japs, they'll eventually figure out how to ask the villagers if they know where we are?"

"Probably."

"They'll take 'em straight here, and we'll lose the outpost. Then they'll take 'em to Mubo, and we'll lose that too."

Sergeant Umberson crossed his arms and waited.

Nance scrunched his nose distastefully. "Well," he began and then hesitated, "did you come here to bloody fight or to ninnywhack around the bloody mulberry bush?"

Despite the tone and implication, Willoth couldn't keep from throwing his head back and laughing uproariously.

Umberson shot fire from his eyes but quickly softened, seeing his officer's reaction. Umberson stepped toward Nance and squared up to him. Nance stood ten inches taller, but Umberson's broad shoulders and thick muscled body would cow any sane man. "You watch your mouth, Corporal," he seethed.

Before the two men could come to blows, Willoth got control of his laughter and got to his feet. He rubbed his watering eyes, then pinched the bridge of his nose. His eyes hardened as he stepped between them, and he stared straight into Nance's blue eyes. "If the villagers lead the Nips to us, they'll die alongside them." He searched Nance for any weakness. "I need to know how you feel about that."

Nance tilted his head back and forth, then smiled. "I'm Australian. I joined the bloody NGVRs to kill the enemies of my country. I'll bloody well kill whoever needs killing, Lieutenant."

Willoth slapped his shoulder. "Good man. I'm not sure command is aware of this situation. I'll urge Captain Wilkes to have money sent with the next resupply, but doubt it'll do much good. We're paupers compared with the Japs at this point. If we can't sway the villagers out of the goodness of their hearts, I'm afraid they'll suffer the consequences." He faced Umberson. "We're done ninnywhacking around the mulberry bush...ready the men, Mick. We'll move into the valley and see about killing the enemy."

Umberson gave Nance a scything glare before climbing down the tree to inform the men. With Umberson out of earshot, Willoth faced Nance and drew on his command voice. "You'll watch your tone from now on. You speak to me like that again, and I'll put you on the next plane out of here and you'll scrub shit out of barrels for the rest of the war." He lifted his chin and steadied his gaze on Nance. "Understood?"

Nance gulped. "Understood, sir."

"Excellent. Let's go kill Japs."

Willoth gathered the men. "I wanna patrol near the river and get a closer look at the airfield. We'll bring demos and set up surprises once we find good cover." He pointed at Private Stoneman. "I want you on point, Stony." Corporal Nance reared back as though affronted, and Willoth gave him a warning glare. Umberson looked ready to throttle the NGVR rifleman. Willoth continued. "I don't want any shooting. This is an information-gathering mission. Before we leave, we'll set our traps, but reconnaissance is the priority, which means quiet." He pointed at Nance. "I want you to stay at the observation platform." He handed Nance a handheld radio. "It's tuned to our frequency. If you see anything coming that we can't handle, tell us. Umberson'll show you how to use it."

Nance's face drooped, reminding Willoth of a schoolboy being punished unfairly. Nance took the radio and mumbled, "I know how it works."

They cinched up loose gear, topped off canteens, and moved off the ridge. Stoneman used the same track they'd used three days before, but unlike Nance's nonchalant stroll, he had his weapon ready and he moved as though the enemy waited just around the corner.

Before reaching the bottom, Stoneman moved off the trail and led them toward the river. Since the ambush, the Japanese had varied their patrols unpredictably. They left at odd times, took alternative routes, and moved as though they expected contact.

The jungle thickened as they neared the river. Stoneman's pace slowed as he found ways through. By the time they reached the river's edge, the day had waned past noon.

The silt in the river gave it a milky look and made it difficult to gauge the depth. Nance had assured them they could ford it easily. The only real hindrance came from the deep mud along the barren edges.

Stoneman led them upstream, using the natural cover near the muddy banks. He stopped when he found a good observation point. While the section waited around the base of a large boulder, Stoneman scrambled up and lay on his stomach. After a few minutes, he signaled and Willoth climbed up after him. The viewpoint overlooked a narrow section of river and beyond it, the airstrip.

Willoth pulled out his binoculars and scanned. He could hardly keep the excitement from his voice. "Good job, Stony. This spot's perfect." He pulled out a pad of paper and the nub of a pencil and started sketching. The observation platform on the ridge gave an excellent overall view, but he realized he hadn't been getting the full picture. From here, the airfield started just two hundred yards away. He saw structures and enemy fortifications he hadn't noticed from on high.

Sergeant Umberson spread the rest of the section into a defensive fan. Willoth sketched the layout for nearly an hour before he finally stuffed the pencil and pad of paper back into his pack. Stoneman hadn't moved. He said, "Good position for a sniper. I've seen two officers already."

Willoth nodded and glanced at his best point man. They'd all mimicked the NGVR men's use of natural camouflage to break up their outlines. The leafy wreath sticking from beneath Stoneman's bush hat made him look as though he had long stringy hair. Willoth bent to look up at the ridge. He looked for the observation post but couldn't see it. "I don't think this boulder's viewable from the platform, but you're right. We should remember this spot."

The handheld radio squawked. Willoth cursed silently,

took it from his pack, and keyed the mic. "Got something?" he asked.

Nance's voice came through tinny and scratched with static. "Jap patrol crossed the river downstream from the airfield. Moving upstream. Over."

Willoth keyed the mic. "Roger. We're leaving now. Out." He whispered to the others, "Jap patrol just crossed the river and is heading our way. Time to leave." Stoneman nodded, and the radio squawked again. Willoth scowled. Nance's lack of radio silence might give them away. He thought about turning it off and stuffing it back into his pack, but keyed the mic instead. "What the bloody hell is it?"

Even through the static, Willoth noticed Nance's voice had taken on a more strained tone. "Japs are coming fast. I think they know you're there."

Willoth felt his face flush, and he lifted his head to look downstream, but thick brush and trees blocked his view. "How the hell...?" He stuffed his binoculars into his pack and wondered if perhaps they'd seen the lens reflection of the binoculars. He'd been careful, but what else could it be? He pushed himself backward off the boulder, and Stoneman followed. Willoth hissed to Umberson, "Nance says Japs know we're here. They're coming fast." Umberson nodded, waiting for more. Willoth noticed Private Blanche nearby holding an anti-personnel mine. "Arm that thing and place it around here somewhere. Stony, get us outta here."

Blanche stepped forward and got to work, gingerly placing, arming, and covering the sinister device. To a layperson, it looked like a discarded tin can. Once assembled and armed, a passing animal or boot would set off the hair trigger. The ensuing explosion, although loud, was designed to maim rather than kill.

Stoneman took point and headed upstream. When they'd

gone thirty yards, Blanche rejoined them. Stoneman led them away from the river's edge. He moved fast.

Willoth caught up to Umberson and got his attention. "Tell Stony to find us a good ambush spot. I don't want to lead them back to the ridge." Umberson nodded and trotted forward. An explosion made them all flinch and crouch. Willoth looked back the way they'd come. Unless an animal had tripped the explosive, the Japanese were close. A shrill scream pierced the jungle, and Willoth pushed the nearest man forward. "The Nips are closer than I thought. Move out."

They ran, not caring about leaving a track. A thick layer of leaves and vines covered the ground. A skilled tracker wouldn't have trouble following them, but Willoth doubted the Japanese had one of those...unless they used native help. His blood ran cold at the thought. If the villagers led the enemy soldiers, they'd die in the ambush alongside their masters. Despite his rough talk to Nance, he didn't relish killing native villagers. He doubted anything good would come of it, and it might anger them enough to join the Japanese.

Stoneman led them to the edge of a small field of tall kunai grass. He crouched, and the others spread out in a defensive ring. Willoth assessed the field and made up his mind quickly. "Take us through. We'll set up on the other side. If they follow, we'll hit them and move off fast."

The troopers pushed their rolled-up shirtsleeves down to cover their bare arms. The edges of the grass were as sharp and unyielding as knife blades. They couldn't do anything about their exposed legs. They pushed into the field, careful to weave through sideways and step onto the grass's base whenever possible. It left an easy trail to follow, but if the enemy followed them this far, it wouldn't matter.

They made it through but, despite their best efforts, exhibited fresh, razor-thin cuts on their hands, legs, and faces. Sweat dripped into the micro-wounds, making them cringe. Willoth pointed at a nearby tree and clapped his Bren man, Private Weathers, on the shoulder and ordered, "Up there. We'll be able to see the field. Set the gun up there." Weathers nodded and moved to the base of the tree. He extended the weapon's bipod. Willoth said, "Rest of you, spread out." Staff Sergeant Umberson directed traffic, but they knew their jobs and were soon hidden and ready to take on all-comers.

Willoth settled in beside Umberson and adjusted himself until he had an unobstructed view of the field. Their position was a few meters higher than the field, giving them a wide open killing ground. He pointed to the right. "If the Japs smell a trap and try to flank us, we'll be in trouble." Umberson nodded his agreement. Willoth ordered, "Extend four men to that side. If it comes to it, we'll bound past them, then cover their withdrawal."

Umberson nodded, got to his feet, and made the change. He returned a few minutes later. "I put Blanche, Brewster, Rickey, and Glandon over there," he whispered.

Willoth nodded, "Good. Now we wait."

A half hour later, Umberson tapped Willoth's leg and pointed. Willoth had just about convinced himself that the Japanese hadn't the stomach to pursue them. He cursed his bad luck. Japanese soldiers emerged at the edge of the field and crouched. Umberson leaned close and whispered, "They're using villagers."

Willoth peered through leaves and branches and saw what Umberson saw, two natives motioning into the field of kunai grass. "Shit," he seethed. The natives gestured emphatically, but the Japanese didn't move into the field. Willoth willed them to cross, but an officer motioned half of them to move around the edge. "They smelled the trap."

Umberson nodded his camouflaged head. "Guess it was too obvious."

Willoth knew he was right. He should've used the time the booby trap gave them to get the hell outta there. Instead, he was having to take on an alerted enemy attacking from two sides. He didn't dwell on it. He ordered, "Take three more troopers and join the others. We'll engage the ones crossing the field. I'll have to engage them before they make it across. The Bren has a good field of fire from here." Umberson nodded and moved off, tapping troopers as he hustled to join the right flank.

Willoth crawled to Weathers manning the Bren. He whispered, "Fire on my command. Hit 'em hard, but be ready to shift right. We may have to punch through the right flank."

Weathers nodded and pulled the primer back slowly, then settled into the stock and sighted down the barrel. Willoth put his rifle to his shoulder and adjusted his sights minutely. The Japanese moved into the field in a single file line, following their trail. It would be a massacre. He took his eyes off the sights and searched for the other group, but he only caught glimpses of movement. He refocused on the soldiers crossing the field.

The lead man neared the end of the field, only fifty yards away. Willoth kept his barrel on the fourth man back. He moved and acted like an NCO. The officer had moved around the flank with the bulk of his men.

When the lead man stepped from the grass, Willoth pressured the trigger, and his rifle bucked in his hand. A puff of dust erupted from the NCO's chest, and his mouth opened as he fell sideways and out of sight. Without conscious thought,

Willoth worked the bolt and found another target. More rifles fired. He noticed the lead enemy soldier was down and writhing.

Weathers opened fire with the Bren and cut a long swath of death through the Japanese ranks. Men dropped, cut down before they could dive for cover. Willoth fired at a diving soldier, but his round buzzed harmlessly past his leg. He worked the bolt and fired into the area his target had gone. Weathers continued sweeping the field with deadly fire.

Willoth got to his knees and yelled, "Move right." Weathers continued firing through his magazine, covering the others as they pulled back to the right flank. Willoth ran to Umberson's side and threw himself behind a downed log. "They won't be coming from the front," he said excitedly.

The chatter of the Bren gun stopped, and Weathers and Sparkingham came running up the hill with wide eyes. Willoth motioned to where Weathers should go. Weathers thumped onto his belly, extended the Bren's long barrel, and rested the bipod on the soft ground. Willoth pointed back down the hill. "Watch the field, Sparky. Don't want any surprises." Sparkingham nodded and moved back the way he'd come and tucked into cover.

Umberson hissed, "There they are." Willoth saw flashes of movement. Rifles barked, and Weathers fired off a quick burst. The sparse jungle provided little cover for the Japanese. They threw themselves into what they could find. The commandos' bullets chased them. Willoth inserted a fresh ten-round magazine and searched for more targets. He saw rifle barrels, gun smoke, and muzzle flashes. He fired to keep their heads down but knew they had to break contact soon. They didn't have enough ammunition for an extended fight, and the Japanese might be reinforced at any moment.

"We've gotta break contact, Mick. Bound 'em uphill."

Umberson nodded and rolled to his knees. "Team One move, Team Two covering fire!"

Bullets ripped from below, and Sparkingham yelled a moment later, "Japs coming up!" He punctuated his yell: "Throwing grenade!" Willoth turned in time to see the small orb flying downhill and disappearing into the brambles. A second later a blast of fire, dust, and debris rolled from the area. Sparkingham calmly fired over and over, working the bolt action smoothly until he'd expended his magazine.

Team One moved a few meters before withering fire forced them down. Willoth recognized the woodpecker-like sound of a Japanese machine gun. "They brought a fucking machine gun!" he yelled. Explosions rocked the area, and he felt the heat from the blasts roll over him. "Shit! Grenades."

Weathers yelled, "Reloading!"

Willoth yelled, "Hit 'em with grenades, then take off!" Willoth pulled his only grenade off his belt, armed it, and chucked it as far as he could before dropping back down. His brief glimpse showed multiple muzzle flashes and smoke.

They were up and running before the grenades exploded. Bullets whacked into trees and whizzed over their heads with vicious snaps. The Japanese machine gun faltered for a few seconds, and Willoth hoped a lucky grenade had silenced it, but his hopes were dashed when it opened fire again and sent a volley of bullets through the trees. They threw themselves to the ground. The volume of fire was too intense.

Willoth's mind reeled. Their ammunition supply dwindled with each shot, and the only resupply involved a day's trek all the way to the village of Mubo. Sergeant Umberson stared at him for orders. The volley of bullets filling the air seemed surreal. He yelled, "Stay down! They can't keep this up forever. Save your ammunition. Wait for them to reload."

Sparkingham slithered his way to Willoth's side. "I got a few of 'em down there, but there might be more."

Willoth nodded. "Keep an eye on it." Sparkingham grew up on the wrong side of the tracks, where he'd been forced to fight for his right to exist. His calmness under fire came from long experience. He simply nodded and kept sighting down his barrel.

Weathers lifted his head, attempting to pinpoint the enemy machine gun. Bullets ripped into the barrel of the Bren and wrenched it from his hands. He yelled in agony as two of his fingers broke with loud snaps. He pulled the Bren out of harm's way, but not before more rounds splintered the stock and dented the breech. He threw it behind him in frustration and clasped his hand. "Bren gun's out of bloody business." He grimaced and yelled, "Fuck off, Tojo!"

Willoth shook his head. "That makes things harder," he yelled in frustration. He looked behind them. The jungle that way thickened, and he wasn't sure they'd be able to push through it at all, but they couldn't move up or they'd be slaughtered. He slapped Umberson's shoulder and pointed, "We've gotta retreat straight back. Push through the thicket."

Umberson looked skeptically at the forty yards of relatively open jungle they'd need to cross before hitting the thicker section. He licked his lips nervously, then nodded. "Our only choice."

Willoth yelled over the din of enemy fire, "We'll do it by teams."

Umberson turned to give the order when the enemy machine gun suddenly stopped firing. Willoth figured they were reloading. Now would be the perfect time to leave. He heard yelling, and shots from a different direction rang out. Incoming fire dropped off to a trickle. He exchanged a glance with Umberson and held up a finger, telling him to wait.

Willoth lifted his head and peeked. He glimpsed Japanese soldiers turned away, firing their rifles behind them and yelling to one another in panicked confusion. A long gout of flame erupted among them, and they screamed and scattered. One soldier ran straight at Willoth, flinging his fire-wreathed arms wildly. Willoth shot him in the chest and he dropped, and the fire swept over the rest of his body. More commandos rose and fired into the chaos. The Japanese broke and ran, disappearing into the jungle.

Willoth heard a familiar voice yelling at their backs.

"Come back here, you bleeding sawed-off runts!"

Willoth raised his voice to Umberson, "Saved by Corporal Nance and his blokes." He shook his head, "We'll never hear the end of this."

5

POSITIONING

It took Lieutenant Willoth and his men three days to get from their overlook position near the airfield back to Wau. Besides Private Weathers's broken fingers, Private Blanche received a bloody head wound from a Japanese bullet's near miss. They'd gotten off easy. If not for Corporal Nance and his NGVRs charging and hurling Molotov cocktails into the midst of the Japanese, things would've been far worse.

Willoth delivered his detailed sketches of the airfield's defenses and relayed what he'd learned about the natives living in Salamaua. Two days later, he and the other section leaders were called into HQ. Colonel Fleay and Major Murdock stood in front waiting for them to take their seats.

Fleay started things off. "A sizable naval force has left Rabaul Harbor and is heading toward Lae. The Americans and our flyboys have been harassing them all the way, but they don't have enough firepower to completely stop them. They're expected to land tomorrow with at least half the troops they left with. We expect them to push inland from Lae and solidify their hold upon the Markham Valley. There's nothing stopping them from moving into our valley once they do...

except us. We also expect them to send troops south to reinforce Salamaua." He looked squarely at Willoth and continued. "Third Section gave them a bloody nose, and the NGVRs that stayed behind tell us they've stepped up patrols ever since."

Lieutenant Blakely leaned forward and slapped Willoth's back. "Atta boy! You lucky sods." Willoth grinned and shrunk away in mock pain. The other section leaders hooted and hollered their approval.

Major Murdock stepped forward and held up his hands. "All right, all right—at ease." He couldn't keep the grin off his face.

Colonel Fleay's grin look painted on. He clearly didn't like being interrupted. He lifted his chin and waited for the men to settle. "The rest of you will get your chance to give them bloody noses too." He let that hang for a few seconds, bringing the sweltering room to a tense silence. "Before the Jap reinforcements get too comfortable, we're going to hit them." He placed his hands on the table and leaned forward, looking them over. "We have detailed maps of the airfield defenses at Salamaua. We'll hit the airfield and the Jap artillery unit stationed outside Lae simultaneously." A dull murmur of approval moved through the officers. Fleay nodded and stood to his full height. "Major Murdock will fill you in on the details, but consider this a warning order. Command wants us to strike a blow out here, and that's just what we're going to do."

―――――

Returning to the observation area overlooking Salamaua airfield felt like returning to the scene of a crime. Corporal Nance greeted Willoth with a crisp salute that felt sarcastic somehow. "Welcome back, Lieutenant Willoth. I knew you couldn't stay away for long." He gave him a seductive wink. "How was your walk back?"

"Exhausting. Glad Mubo got resupplied, though. We only had to carry full packs from there."

Nance nodded sagely. "Yes, smart thinking."

Again, Willoth felt mocked. "Hear the Nips have kept you jumping since we left."

Nance shrugged. "Nothing we can't handle. The booby traps you left for us helped curb their interest."

Willoth smiled at that, knowing the perverse joy Nance derived from causing Japanese soldiers' pain and suffering. "Have they filled you in on what's happening?" Willoth asked.

Nance nodded, but his mouth turned down at the corners, dragging his unkempt beard along with it. "Yes. Unfortunately, we're ordered back to Bulol."

Willoth was surprised. The NGVRs hadn't been talked about in the plan, but he assumed they'd play a role in the upcoming mission. "All the way to Bulol?"

"Captain Grimerson's orders. We are to leave as soon as you blokes arrive and are made comfortable."

Willoth extended a hand, and they shook. "Comfortable? Not a simple task. Well, I'm sad to see you go. You saved our asses the last time we tangled with the Japs."

Nance stroked his beard. "That was a fine day. A proper Jap-barby, it was."

Willoth remembered seeing and smelling the burning Japanese. The sight haunted his dreams occasionally. Native porters appeared from the trail. They carried logs strung with full canvas bags hanging nearly to the ground. Nance's eyes lit up. "More toys?" he asked.

Willoth stepped aside to let them pass. "Yeah. Explosives,

mostly. We're going to give the Japs a loud wake-up call if we can get close enough."

Nance didn't take his eyes off the bundles as the porters lowered them to the ground carefully. He tilted his head. "Maybe there'll be leftovers." He looked at Willoth beseechingly. "Leave some here if there are. We'll be back before too long."

Willoth shrugged. "We have just enough. Doubt there'll be leftovers." He pointed to another group of porters. Some carried mortar tubes, some carried the base plates, and others hauled the mortar shell boxes. "Perhaps they'll let you play with those when we're done."

Nance rubbed his hands together, then covered his mouth, as though Willoth had offered him the queen's crown. "Oh, would I ever love to get my hands on one of those."

"Jesus, Nance." He shook his head. "You're a real piece of work." Willoth slapped him on the back. "Before you go, show me what the Nips have been up to."

Nance tore his attention away from the mortars and led Willoth up the old tree to the platform. Willoth scrambled up and noticed the hammock missing. He'd hoped to try it out in a more reasonable area closer to the ground.

Nance plopped down on the edge of the platform, dangling his feet, and Willoth joined him. Willoth gazed into the green and brown abyss a hundred feet below. He pulled back before getting dizzy. Nance barely noticed the precipitous drop.

The sun hung low in the sky, casting shadows over the river and the airfield beyond. Nance pointed. "They've been mostly patrolling along the western and southern edges. They cross the river daily and move through the area where we fought them."

Willoth brought his binoculars to his eyes. He scanned the

airfield slowly. It looked exactly how he remembered. "We'll be hitting it from the north. That's where most of the buildings are. Hopefully, we'll be able to get close enough to plant the explosives and find cover from the blasts." Nance nodded, and Willoth let his binoculars dangle from his neck. "Too bad there aren't any Zeros. They'd be a fat target."

Nance punched his arm, and his eyes widened with excitement. "Almost forgot to tell you." He pointed east. "Look that way—on the water about forty-five degrees from the tip of the airfield."

Willoth put the binoculars up and saw a well-camouflaged Jap floatplane pulled onto the beach. He adjusted the focus. "Hello, beautiful," he cooed. "How long has she been there?"

"Just came in this afternoon. Probably leaves in the morning."

"How d'you know that?"

"He took on fuel. It took a long time, so I figure he was low and had probably come a long way. He'll need to rest. Doubt he'd leave this close to nightfall."

Willoth lowered his binocs and beamed. "Well, if he's still there before dawn, he'll wish he wasn't."

The NGVRs lingered and finally left around midnight. Willoth enjoyed their company, despite their eccentricities. Before leaving, Nance told the officers everything he could about the Japanese defenses and their patrolling habits and routes.

The Third Platoon planned to leave for their jump-off points at 0200, but after the NGVRs faded into the darkness on their journey to Bulol, Captain Wilkes moved the timeline up. "No sense waiting. No one's going to sleep anyway. Let's kick this off."

Willoth and the other section leads didn't complain. They had carefully spread the gear to each man, and everyone knew their jobs. Waiting around for two more hours made little sense to anyone.

The night sky was mostly clear of clouds, and a half moon lit up their surroundings. They moved from the ridge toward the river and the airfield in a long, snaking single-file line. Nance assured them that the Japanese hadn't been sending patrols out at night. The Japanese were operating with a skeleton crew after losing troops to booby traps and ambushes. Despite that, the platoon moved carefully.

Once on the flats, they moved upstream, avoiding the mud of the alluvial floodplain. At a narrow section of river, the scouts waded across the knee-deep water and secured the far bank. The rest of the platoon crossed four at a time. The troopers spread into a defensive circle while the officers gathered in the shadows and huddled around Captain Wilkes. His eyes sparkled in the diluted moonlight. "All right, this is where we part ways." He looked at the luminescent dials on his watch. "Synchronize watches. It's exactly 0150 hours...now." He refocused on the men staring at him. "We'll hit them at 0500 hours. You've got plenty of time, so take it slow. If they spot any of us, the gig's up." He turned toward Lieutenant Mounters. "Be ready to cover us with your mortars. I'll leave it up to you where to set up, but make sure you have a clear route of egress. Ten rounds, then you pack up and get the hell outta here."

Lieutenant Mounters's lips pursed in a thin line, and he nodded. "Yes, sir."

Wilkes grinned and looked each man in the eye. "Good luck. The rally point's back across the river." He pointed the way they'd come. "See you in a few hours."

Willoth watched Wilkes turn his back and join Lt. Wilson's

First Section. Wilson was the youngest and most inexperi-
enced officer. Willoth exchanged a glance with Lt. Blakely.
Blakely nodded, and Willoth returned the gesture. He thought
Blakely looked more scared than excited.

Willoth's experience over the past three weeks made him
and his Third Section the old hands of the platoon. Willoth
still felt as green as everyone else, but the looks of admiration
couldn't be denied. He'd been tested, and he'd survived. The
other officers didn't know for sure how they'd react when the
bullets flew. A few noncoms and enlisted men had tangled
with the Germans in Africa, but barring Captain Wilkes, none
of the other officers had seen combat.

Willoth and his men stayed put until the others faded
from sight and sound. The other sections headed north
toward structures and enemy bunkers closer to the village.
Willoth's targets were the buildings around the airfield itself.

He tapped Private Stoneman's shoulder. "Take us downstream, Stony." Stoneman gave a curt nod and moved east
toward the southern section of the runway. The night sounds
of insects and calls from wild animals rose above the burbling
river. The moon hung low but bathed the area with a grayish
light. Stoneman kept them in the shadowy darkness as much
as possible.

They finally arrived at the edge of the clearing in front of
the airfield. The Japanese, along with help from the natives,
had cleared out the brush around the airfield, leaving a sixty-
foot buffer zone.

They stopped, and the men spread out. Willoth checked
his watch. He had plenty of time to settle in and watch. He
studied the target from the cover of the brush.

Two enemy soldiers stood close together near the base of a
makeshift control tower. The simple structure reminded him
of the observation platform on the ridge. It comprised a long

plank of wood with a rickety railing perched on stilts and extending thirty feet up. The canvas roof was covered with camouflage netting and looked sturdy enough to withstand the sudden and violent rain that plagued the area.

It, along with a barracks on the eastern corner and the bamboo revetments along the edges, was his primary target. He couldn't see the floatplane from this angle, but he hadn't heard it take off. He wondered if the pilot slept in the barracks or the nearby flight operations building. He wiped the sweat from his brow and wondered if it would be possible to take the pilot alive. That would be an intelligence boon. He sighed and checked his watch again. He estimated the moon would sink below the horizon by the time they moved out. Now all he had to do was wait.

Major Murdock and the men of First and Second Platoon watched their target in the gray light of the moon. The perfectly square concrete building looked out of place against the lush jungle hillside. The barrel of the Japanese artillery piece stuck out obscenely from the front slot. The barrel could traverse 180 degrees from west to east, allowing it to shell targets inland as easily as out to sea.

The major pointed and whispered, "You'll take your section down this ravine and blow the bridge." Lt. Muncey, leading Second Section of Second Platoon, nodded. He knew the plan like the back of his hand. If Murdock wanted to burn off nervous energy and tell him his job again, so be it. Murdock continued. "You must drop it, or the reinforcements from Lae will arrive too quickly and they'll shoot us in the back."

Muncey nodded again. "Yes, sir. I understand. We'll get it done."

Murdock slapped his section leader's shoulder. "I know." Muncey thought that was the end of it, but Murdock continued. "Timing's everything. As soon as we blow the gun, you blow the bridge, then get back to the rally point."

Muncey folded his arms across his powerful chest. "Yes, sir."

Murdock looked at his watch. "I didn't know time could move this slow. It's worse than waiting for news of a firstborn."

Muncey grimaced. "You have a family, sir?"

Murdock nodded absently.

"Thought the commando companies tried to choose cadre without many family attachments, sir."

Murdock tilted his head. "That's true. I'm divorced. My ex took my boy to New Zealand. Bloody Kiwi asshole's raising my son now." His face changed from worried to angry in an instant. "Guess the company didn't consider that an attachment."

Muncey didn't know what to say. He murmured, "That's rough."

"I fantasized about meeting the sod out here on the battlefield." He mimicked shooting a pistol with his hand. "Lot can happen during the heat of battle." Muncey gave him a sardonic grin. Murdock shrugged. "But the coward's not even man enough to fight for his country. Got himself listed as an essential worker to the war effort."

"Pity."

"Yes, quite." He shook his head, coming back to the present. He checked his watch again, and his command voice returned. "We step off in an hour. Let your men know."

6

RAID!

Lieutenant Willoth wiped the condensation from his wristwatch. The fireworks would start in ten minutes. He signaled for Stoneman to lead them from cover. Stoneman nodded, adjusted his pack, and stepped from the trees. The moon had set and with it the dim light. The two guards still stood shoulder to shoulder near the control tower. They talked in low murmurs; occasionally one would laugh.

Willoth assigned Stoneman and Sparkingham to them. He'd considered ways to do the job quietly but didn't think they could get close enough for knife work. They'd have to be taken out with rifles.

Stoneman led them along a low drainage ditch that paralleled the airstrip. When he'd gone three hundred feet, he stopped and crouched. Sparkingham crept up beside him. They left the safety of the ditch and moved toward the airstrip on their bellies.

Willoth followed and lay beside them. The dim outlines of the guards seemed very close. The skilled riflemen would have easy shots. Willoth pulled the sleeve back from his watch. He held up three fingers; three minutes until the northern forces attacked.

With one minute to go, Willoth tapped Sparkingham, and he in turn tapped Stoneman. They took aim down their Lee-Enfield rifle sights and settled into position. Willoth glanced at the others. They crouched in the ditch. The first five men had their packs off and held modified sticky grenade bombs. The others held their rifles at the ready. They would provide covering fire while the bombers moved forward and hurled their bombs into buildings and airplane revetments.

Willoth returned his eyes to his watch. He whispered a countdown, starting at ten seconds. Despite the countdown, Willoth jumped at the simultaneous crack of the rifles. Both enemy guards jolted and dropped into the shadows at the base of the tower. Willoth waved his men forward. "Go, go, go," he said just above a whisper.

The men in the ditch ran toward the tower. Stoneman and Sparkingham had already chambered their next rounds and, keeping their rifles on the downed guards, moved forward. One commando chucked his hissing sticky grenade onto the control tower platform. The heavy bomb thumped loudly, and the sticky grease kept it from rolling off. The other bombers sprinted toward the first revetments. The covering riflemen kept pace, watching the shadows for an enemy response.

Willoth glanced at the still bodies lying at the base of the tower. He could only see their silhouettes, but they didn't pose a threat. He ran past, watching the barracks building intently. So far, the rifle shots hadn't gotten anyone's attention. He doubted that could last much longer. His men hurled bombs into two revetments and continued charging toward the operations building.

Willoth heard someone shout. A flash near the barracks building caught his attention. The unmistakable sound of a bullet smacking into wood made him flinch. He saw Brewster and Blanche kneel, aim, and fire toward the muzzle flash. Willoth kept running. The bombs had long fuses, but they couldn't afford to get pinned down, or they'd be caught in their own blasts.

He saw silhouettes and shapes near the buildings. He crouched and pulled his rifle to his shoulder. Someone ducked around the corner of the barracks building. He wondered if it could be the pilot. Would he make a break for his aircraft? A flash sparked, and Willoth returned fire and worked the bolt action, then fired again.

The first bomb exploded behind him, and he felt the heat wave and concussion sweep up his back. Flames, smoke, and flying debris filled the air. The control tower ceased to exist. They didn't have enough spare explosives to test the makeshift bombs, so they didn't quite know what they were dealing with. The men who thought they hadn't used enough TNT were clearly wrong.

He yelled, "Keep moving!" He took off running, keeping his eyes on the corner of the barracks. His men continued firing as the bombers sprinted toward the buildings at the far end of the field.

The second explosion rocked him. He kept running. The blast turned night into day momentarily, and he saw shapes darting this way and that. He wanted to stop and fire but realized the next explosion would come at any moment, and the more distance he put between himself and it, the better.

He saw Sergeant Umberson running just ahead. He called out to him, "Let's get to the floatplane, Mick."

Umberson glanced back, and his face lit up as the third explosion demolished another revetment. He gripped his floppy jungle hat and yelled through gritted teeth, "I'm with you."

They angled to the right, away from the barracks and operations building. Umberson yelled at two nearby troopers. "Brewster, Blanche—come with us!" They veered away from the charging bomb throwers and fell in with them. They sprinted toward the darkness beyond the buildings.

Willoth watched two men hurl one bomb apiece into the operations building. He cringed. That much firepower would probably demolish the nearby barracks building too. A brief firefight broke out near the barracks. The supporting commandos stopped and unleashed a steady stream of bullets. Willoth didn't like it. "Umberson! Get the men pulled back. Forget about the barracks for now. Get them away from the building." Umberson turned back toward the firefight, screaming orders.

Willoth and his two troopers continued sprinting but angled away from the buildings. Soon the firefight sounded distant as they entered the thin jungle separating the beach from the airfield. Darkness once again closed in, and they slowed their headlong charge to a trot. Brewster and Blanche moved ahead and spread out. Willoth searched the darkness, but his eyes still had spots from the massive explosions.

He caught sight of the edge of the sea and scanned left, hoping to spot the floatplane. He instinctively dropped flat onto his belly when the world behind him suddenly erupted in flame and noise. He kept his hand on his bush hat as the concussion and heat made the trees wave as though in a brief, hellish wind.

He caught sight of the floatplane reflecting the flames licking the edge of the jungle. Movement near the water caught his eye. Someone darted up the pontoon, then onto the wing. Blanche and Brewster stared behind them at the massive results of the explosion. Willoth pointed at the plane. "Someone's there. On the plane." Both troopers tore their eyes from the conflagration and focused on the bobbing aircraft. "We've gotta stop him."

Willoth got to his feet and trotted toward the aircraft. The closer he got, the better he could see a figure on the wing. It was the pilot. A surge of adrenaline coursed through his body at the prospect of capturing the pilot and the plane. He sprinted onto the beach.

In the glow from the flames, he saw the pilot spin in his direction. Willoth kept running straight and fast. The pilot pulled a pistol. Willoth dove sideways just as the Japanese pilot fired. The bullet missed by a wide margin, but Willoth stayed down and crawled toward the edge of the jungle. More shots, and this time he heard the whiz-crack as a bullet passed over his head and smacked the sand. Rifle fire from Blanche and Brewster ended the pistol shots.

Willoth watched the pilot slip and fall off the wing. He landed hard on the pontoon, then slid into the water. Willoth got to his feet and trotted toward the plane with his rifle ready. Blanche and Brewster joined on either side. Brewster asked, "You okay, Lieutenant?"

Willoth nodded and kept his rifle aimed at the dark water beneath the plane. "I'm fine. Careful. He went into the water." Blanche moved a few yards right, toward the edge of the water, keeping his rifle on his shoulder. "If he's alive, try to capture him," Willoth ordered.

They slowed as they approached the plane. It looked much bigger than he expected it to be. There was no sign of the pilot, but the blood streak near the cockpit told them he'd been hit at least once. They stood with their rifles at their shoulders, searching the water. The sounds of gunfire from the airfield ended with one last rifle shot. The crackling of burning buildings mixed with the lapping water along the plane's pontoons made it almost idyllic.

The sudden eruption of water and the pained scream of the pilot coming up for air nearly made Willoth jump out of his skin. The Japanese pilot stood in waist-deep water. His pistol wavered in his hand. Willoth watched the pistol barrel rise toward his chest, but before Willoth could pull the trigger, Blanche and Brewster fired simultaneously. The pilot's chest spouted gouts of blood. The pilot's head smashed into the metal pontoon with a dull thump before he slid into the dark water.

Willoth stood there, trying to get control of his breathing. Brewster waded in and dragged the lifeless pilot's body onto the beach. Blanche kept his rifle trained on the body and asked, "You all right, sir?"

Willoth nodded. "I thought that was that. He had me beat."

Blanche shrugged. "Wounded? Firing a pistol?" He slapped Willoth's shoulder. "He woulda missed by a mile."

Staff Sergeant Umberson and a few other troopers burst onto the beach. Relief flooded Umberson's face, seeing his officer alive and well. "Orders, sir?"

Willoth ordered, "Search the body and the plane. He might be a courier. Did the barracks survive?"

Umberson shook his head. "The blast from the other building set it on fire. It's a bloody inferno." He couldn't keep the joy from his voice.

Men scrambled up the side of the plane. Private Glandon held a bag over his head and called out jubilantly, "Here's something."

Brewster stood from searching the body. "Pilot's still in his skivvies. Unless he's got something shoved up his arse, he's clean."

Private Rickey jibed, "Check it, mate. You never know."

Brewster swore, "Fuck off, Rickey."

Willoth ordered, "Put a grenade in the cockpit, and let's get the bloody hell outta here."

Glandon handed him an expensive-looking leather satchel. Willoth unclipped the latch and saw reams of paper and folders. He re-clasped the brass clips and slung it cross-ways over his back.

Brewster yelled, "Fire in the hole."

Willoth ducked, and the cockpit blew with sparks, flame, and smoke. "Weathers, put some .303 into the engine."

Weathers turned his replacement Bren toward the engine compartment and fired away. Chunks flew off, and the plane's metal skin sparked and twinkled. The fire from the grenade took on new life, and soon it burned lustily.

They trotted past the burning buildings, taking stock of their handiwork. They got to the edge of the river and made their crossing quickly, then veered upstream toward the rally point. Willoth beamed. No matter how everyone else fared, his mission was an unmitigated success.

Major Murdock glanced at his watch. He had planned to hit the artillery bunker at 0430 hours, but getting past the marsh-land bordering the Markham River had taken longer than expected. From his perch the night before, the approach looked simple enough, but once they were in it, their progress slowed to a crawl. He had little chance of keeping the timeline he'd set out for himself. Now, he only hoped to make it before dawn.

He thought he heard the distant rumble of explosions, but out here, it could just as easily have been thunder, or even a spewing volcano. They finally reached the high ground over-looking the gun emplacement. In the distance, the sleepy port town of Lae was dark. He knew a sizable force of Japanese lived there, but he saw nothing but darkened huts and native outrigger canoes scattered along the beach.

The road snaked up from town, crossed the Markham River, and led directly to the artillery bunker. It passed on by and continued up the valley but turned to little more than a track before reaching Nadzab Airfield further northwest. The Japanese had been improving the road, but it was no small feat out here. The monsoon rains—still a few months off—had a way of spoiling construction projects, not to mention the sweltering heat.

The platoons halted and spread out in a defilade, out of sight from the bunker or Lae. Major Murdock checked his watch again. The sun would be up in less than thirty minutes. Already the hints of dawn spread across the region. The men looked to him. He'd planned the raid. They were already well past the stated timeline. Attacking in broad daylight would be risky. He looked at the sky and made his decision. "Let's get this done."

The men looked relieved. They knew the mission and didn't need direction, just permission. First Platoon split off downhill toward the bridge. They stayed in the ravine, working their way quickly and taking advantage of the last vestiges of darkness.

Murdock joined his two other officers on the lip of the ravine and watched the concrete bunker. They would approach from the left side, near the wooded hillside. It would keep them out of sight most of the way. The Japanese had cut back the trees and vegetation the last seventy feet in front of the bunker to provide a killing ground. That would be where the commandos would be most exposed. He whispered, "Let's get going. We need to take advantage of the darkness."

The officers nodded and waved the men forward. The

commandos kept their intervals and moved left, keeping low and moving silently. Major Murdock unslung his rifle and followed. He was old enough to be most of the troopers' father, but he prided himself on his physical fitness. More than a few of them had underestimated him during training exercises back in Victoria and been embarrassed as he marched or ran them into the ground.

They kept to the shadows until they reached the edge of the jungle. A great green wall extended nearly straight up, only a few yards from their position. They pushed in until they couldn't go any further, then moved toward the bunker. The sky lightened noticeably. A trooper pointed south. In the far distance, a plume of black smoke curled into the morning sky. Murdock's resolve stiffened. The rest of the company had done its job hitting the airfield at Salamaua, and now it was their turn to do theirs.

He reached into his pack and pulled out the handheld walkie-talkie. They had endless trouble with the bigger radio sets, but these smaller units, although not as powerful, worked surprisingly well. He flipped it on, making sure the volume was on low. He'd need to know if First Platoon ran into problems.

Their pace slowed as they neared the section of open ground. Half the bunker shone in the morning light, and half remained shrouded by shadow. Murdock strained to see any enemy soldiers.

Second Section spread out, went prone, and used their packs to stabilize their rifles. They'd stay back while First and Third Sections made the assault. Murdock desperately wanted to lead the assault, but he'd promised Colonel Fleay he'd stay with the covering section so he could direct them better.

He pushed the bar on the side of the radio and whispered, "Pushing now. Out." A few seconds passed before a quick double-click answered back. He nodded toward Lieutenant Franks and Lieutenant Quigley. They waved their men forward and, keeping as low as possible, pushed into the open ground.

From his position, the men looked impossibly exposed. He wished they'd been here even a half hour earlier. He shook his head. There was nothing he could do about that now. His breath caught in his throat when he saw a Japanese soldier emerge from the bunker. He turned toward the sea, facing away. Every rifle in Second Section aimed at the man's back. The exposed commandos kept inching forward.

The Japanese soldier undid his pants and pissed into the morning air. Murdock willed the man to keep looking the other way. If he raised the alarm now, he wasn't sure the attack would be successful. The only way to take out the bunker was by surprise. The NGVRs reported there was at least one and possibly two machine guns guarding the bunker.

Murdock suddenly had an overwhelming feeling of impending doom. He'd learned to pay attention to these feelings, and he'd never felt it this strongly before. He hesitated for a moment. His internal warning bells warring against common sense. His men were nearly there. If he called them back now, they'd bring him up on charges. He shunned the feeling to the pit of his stomach, and it burned like dry ice.

The radio suddenly came to life. He heard Lt. Muncey's tinny voice, laced with fear. "Two troop trucks coming up the road. We're not in place yet. Repeat, explosives not set." A second later, a machine gun opened fire from that direction. "They spotted us."

Murdock keyed the radio and ordered, "Get the hell out of there. Repeat—fall back to rally point."

The Japanese soldier yelled and gestured excitedly down the road. More soldiers emerged from the bunker—many more than Murdock thought would be there. One looked his way, and it was as if their eyes locked. The soldier screamed and pointed. Murdock barked, "Open fire!"

The rifles of Second Section fired in quick succession, and he saw a few enemy soldiers fall, but most ran into the safety of the bunker. The sound of gunfire near the bridge continued. Murdock stepped forward and yelled at the exposed troopers, "Throw grenades and retreat! Now!" He leveled his own rifle and fired into the slot in the concrete. He didn't have a target, but he hoped to keep their heads down. Second Section continued to pour it on, and the Bren gun finally got into the action. The concrete chipped away, and dust hung in the morning air.

Grenades arced toward the bunker and exploded with dull thumps. NCOs yelled, ordering the men back. The grenades didn't come close to hitting the bunker, but they provided a dense wall of debris and smoke.

Second Section covered their withdrawal with accurate fire, and soon everyone made it back to the initial step-off point. "Fall back, fall back to the rally point!" Murdock yelled, pushing men back. He brought his rifle to his shoulder, seeing movement inside the bunker. He fired and worked the bolt quickly until he'd burned through the ten-round magazine. He quickly inserted another. First and Third Sections were past them. Murdock fired again, then yelled, "Fall back, Second Section! Fall back!"

The men staggered to their knees, put their packs on, and got to their feet. A few fired, covering their comrades, then took off. Murdock urged them to hurry. "Go! Go! Go!"

Staff Sergeant Haynes, his senior NCO, punched his shoulder. "Come on, sir. Time to go. Move it out."

Murdock realized they were the only two remaining. He took one last glance toward the bunker, and his face paled.

The massive barrel of the artillery piece seemed to be aimed directly at him. He pushed Sergeant Haynes down, and he tripped and sprawled into the bushes and brambles. Murdock yelled, "Inco..." but the roar of the gun and the simultaneous impact of the 105mm shell passing through his chest cut off his yell.

Haynes watched from the bushes. One moment the major was there, the next only his smoking legs remained. "Christ almighty," he screamed. He pushed himself to his feet and ran as fast as his legs could carry him.

EPILOGUE

Third Platoon had taken the Japanese by surprise and dealt the garrison at Salamaua a deadly blow. They'd crossed the river and arrived at the rally point with no further enemy contact. A few minutes later, the other sections from Third Platoon arrived. Everyone beamed with their success. Captain Wilkes checked in with the observers left upon the ridge, and they reported no signs of enemy pursuit. The mortar squad broke down their tubes without firing a single shell.

Once back on the ridge, the men spread out, and the officers mounted the platform and took in their handiwork. In the morning light, smoke curled from the still-burning buildings. Soldiers scurried back and forth from the river and the sea carrying buckets of water.

Lieutenant Willoth handed the satchel off to Captain Wilkes, who pulled the papers out and leafed through them. He couldn't read Japanese. "This looks like good stuff. Official seals and signatures all over them." He stuffed them back in the bag and clasped the clips. "I'll get this back to Moresby as soon as we can get it on a plane." He slapped Willoth's shoulder. "Good show, Lieutenant."

Willoth smiled. "Thank you, sir. It was certainly a group effort. Have you heard any news from the Lae operation?"

"Benson heard some radio traffic, but it was garbled. The bits and pieces he picked up..." He paused and scowled. "Well, it didn't go as planned."

Willoth scanned through his binoculars but couldn't see any sign of smoke, which might mark a battle near Lae. "So what now, sir?"

"We'll take the Black Cat Track back to Wau. We'll leave as soon as the men get some food and water."

"Think the Nips will find our little observation post?"

Wilkes waved his bush hat through a swarm of mosquitos. "Not for a while. I don't think they have many men left down there."

"We gave them quite the pasting," Willoth agreed.

"Yes. Too bad there aren't more of us here. We could kick 'em out of there easily. My guess is, they'll send reinforcements from Lae as soon as possible. Then they'll sweep the area." He raised his voice for the other officers to hear. "Get your men fed. We leave in an hour."

Despite the failed Lae mission and the tragic loss of Major Murdock, Lieutenant Colonel Fleay was ecstatic about the successful raid on the airfield. He sent off a message to Moresby telling them of their one-sided victory. He promised the entire company medals for their heroism.

Willoth felt exhausted. The build-up to the mission, the long march there, the actual assault, then the three-day march back left little time for relaxation. He hadn't gotten a full night's sleep in days. It wasn't just the tension from the mission; sleeping outside in New Guinea meant you slept with millions of mosquitos, massive beetles, aggressive ants, deadly centipedes, and poisonous snakes, just to name a few. Now that he sat on a sleeping mat in the relative safety of a thatch hut, the exhaustion hit him like a physical force, and he slept for twelve straight hours.

AFTERWORD

The Japanese suffered a staggering and unexpected defeat because of this historic raid. The Australians destroyed many buildings and reported killing 115 Japanese soldiers at the cost of one man killed and three others lightly wounded. They recovered a satchel of documents from a Japanese pilot spending the night at the airfield. The documents held details for planned construction projects on many islands in the region and became known as, "The Kanga Document."

DARK VALLEY
Tark's Ticks #5

Some missions are FUBAR from the very beginning.

Tarkington and his men are tasked with a long-range reconnaissance mission deep behind enemy lines. But when their
C-47 is shot down, Tark's team must make the perilous trek
through the jungle to a besieged Wau airfield. The airfield is
vital to both the Allies and the Japanese, and soon Tarkington
and his men are embroiled in its defense. To make matters
worse, an American airman has been captured by the nearby
Japanese forces.

Can Tark's Ticks defend the airfield and rescue the downed
aviator? Or will a hostile jungle and determined enemy prove
to be too much?

Get your copy today at
severnriverbooks.com/series/tarks-ticks-wwii-novels

ABOUT THE AUTHOR

Chris Glatte graduated from the University of Oregon with a BA in English Literature and worked as a river guide/kayak instructor for a decade before training as an Echocardiographer. He worked in the medical field for over 20 years, and now writes full time. Chris is the author of multiple historical fiction thriller series, including A Time to Serve and Tark's Ticks, a set of popular WWII novels. He lives in Southern Oregon with his wife, two boys, and ever-present Labrador, Hoover. When he's not writing or reading, Chris can be found playing in the outdoors—usually on a river or mountain.

From Chris:

I respond to all email correspondence.
Drop me a line, I'd love to hear from you!
chrisglatte@severnriverbooks.com

Sign up for Chris Glatte's reader list at
severnriverbooks.com/authors/chris-glatte

Printed in the United States
by Baker & Taylor Publisher Services